5
7/07
22

For my valiant
and
unforgettable
friend,
Charlie Tolchin
—J. V.

For my family and for all families.
May many good things catch you by surprise.
—D. C. B.

Atheneum Books for Young Readers

An imprint of Simon & Schuster Children's Publishing Division

1230 Avenue of the Americas, New York, New York 10020

Book design by Ann Bobo

The text for this book is set in Janson.

The illustrations are rendered in mixed media.

Manufactured in China

First Edition

10 9 8 7 6 5 4 3 2 1

Library of Congress Cataloging-in-Publication Data

Viorst, Judith.

Just in case / by Judith Viorst ; illustrated by Diana Cain Bluthenthal.—1st ed.

p.   cm.

Summary: Charlie likes to be ready for anything, imagining that his house could be flooded or a mermaid might kidnap him, but he learns that it is sometimes good to be unprepared.

ISBN-13: 978-0-689-87164-1

ISBN-10: 0-689-87164-3

[1. Preparedness—Fiction.] I. Bluthenthal, Diana Cain, ill. II. Title.

PZ7 .V816Ju 2005

[E]—dc22   2003026068

Just in case

written by
judith viorst

illustrated by
diana cain
bluthenthal

ginee seo books

atheneum books for young readers

new york   london   toronto   sydney

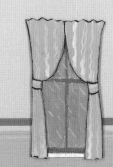

Charlie, whenever it's raining real hard, thinks . . .

"Supposing it rains in the house,

And rains down SO hard

that it makes the furniture float."

So Charlie puts on his waterproof boots
And goggles to cover his eyes.
He puts on his yellow rain hat and yellow rain coat.

Then he opens his special umbrella up

(The one that looks like a frog).

And then he blows up his inflatable plastic boat,
Which will float around with the furniture
Until it's a sunshine-y day.

Charlie knows how to be ready.

And Charlie likes to be ready,

Just in case.

And just in case, when his parents go out

And his favorite sitter can't come,

And the lady who comes to sit is bossy and mean,

So mean that she won't read him storybooks,

And won't let him look at TV,

And won't let him have dessert till he eats every bean,

Charlie is going to make her not glad
That she came to his house to sit
By doing all kinds of weird stuff that she's never seen:

Like washing his feet in the toilet bowl.

Like wearing his shoes on his ears.

Like painting his face a most horrible shade of green.

Then the sitter will phone his mom and his dad.
"Save me from Charlie!" she'll say.

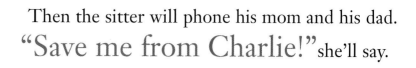

And they will, because Charlie is ready.

Charlie likes to be ready,

Just in case.

And just in case all the food stores are closed,

And stay closed for a really long time,

And there's nothing left to eat except old dirty socks,

Charlie has made a hundred and seventeen
Peanut-butter sandwiches
And wrapped them up nicely and packed them all in a box,
Along with some blueberry yogurt
And crispy crackers (that's for his mom),
And (for his dad) lots of bagels with cream cheese and lox

So there's plenty of food for everyone
Straight through to the middle of May.

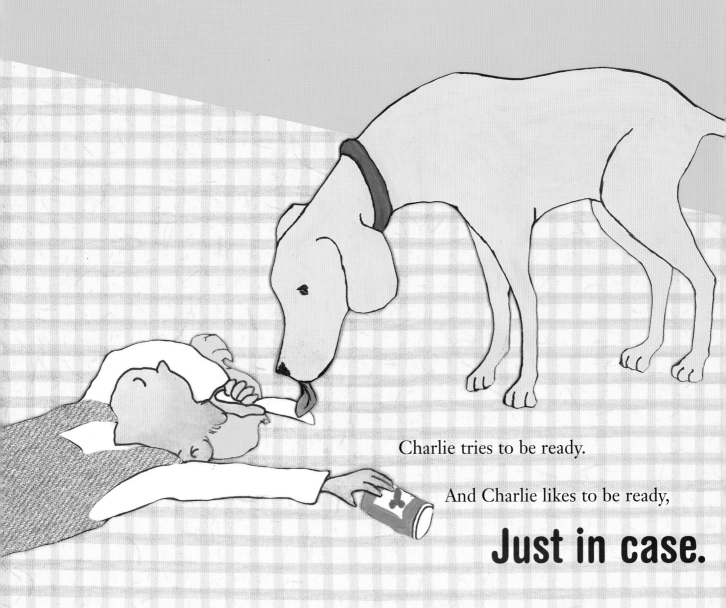

Charlie tries to be ready.

And Charlie likes to be ready,

Just in case.

And sometimes Charlie is lying in bed,

And he's staring right up at the dark,

Long after he's brushed his teeth, washed his face, said a prayer,

And everyone else is deep asleep

Instead of awake and wondering,

"What is that creakity-creak-creak-creak-creak on the stair?"

So Charlie gets up and puts on his cape.
And he puts on his fierce black mask.

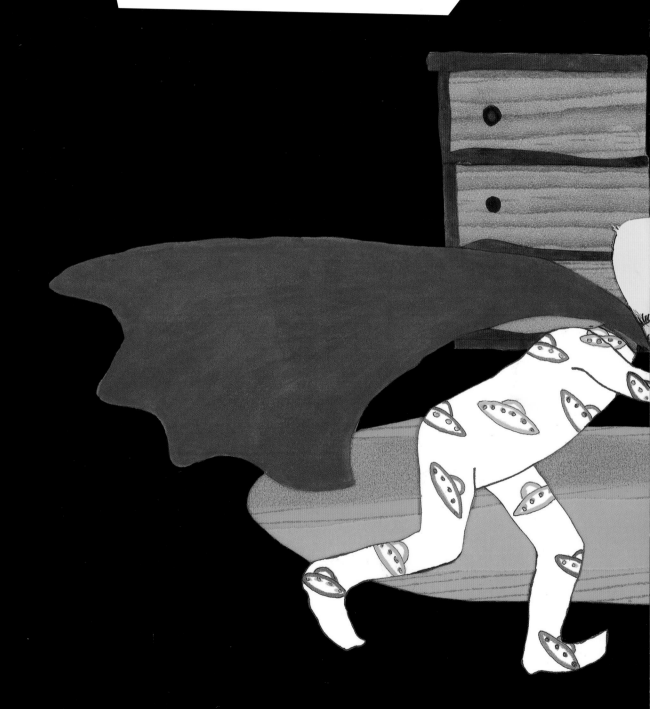

He finds his sword, and he twirls it around in the air.
Then he stands by the door and says, through the door,
In his superhero voice,

"Whoever you are, and whatever you want—beware!"

"Whoever you are—beware!" he says,

Till whoever it is goes away.

Charlie knows how to be ready.

And Charlie likes to be ready,

Just in case.

And just in case, if a lion gets loose

And goes prowling through street after street,

And he prowls onto Charlie's street a little past dawn,

Charlie has started digging a pit.

He will cover it over with leaves,

Which the lion will walk on and —whoosh!—that lion's gone.

And rather than chewing up Charlie for lunch

With his big white pointy teeth,

He'll sit in the pit that Charlie has dug in the lawn,

Till the zoo-keeper tells him, "Get back to the zoo!"

Charlie hopes he'll obey.

But meanwhile, Charlie is ready.

Charlie likes to be ready,

Just in case.

And sometimes Charlie is walking to school,

And he's watching the birds flying south

And worrying maybe a bird's after him instead.

And maybe she'll swoop him up in her beak,

And carry him off to her nest,

And make him eat worms, which is what bird babies are fed.

Or maybe she'll—

Oops!—let him drop, which is why

He took his helmet along

To protect his head if he—

Oops!—should land on his head.

Plus a sleeping bag, if he has to sleep

On a nest made of scratchy twigs,

Which is what, when birds go to bed, they use for a bed.

Plus a parachute, if he's stuck in that nest,

And he doesn't wish to stay.

Because Charlie tries to be ready.

And Charlie likes to be ready,

Just in case.

And sometimes when Charlie's down at the beach,

Building castles and forts in the sand,

He's thinking a mermaid could grab him by his big toe

And pull him far out in the ocean,

So he has taken his rowing oars

And back to the shore, on the mermaid's back, he will row.

Then he'll wrap her up in his fishing net

(For of course he brought a net too)

And throw her back into the sea with one mighty throw,

Telling the mermaid, "Find mermaids, not boys,

The next time that you want to play."

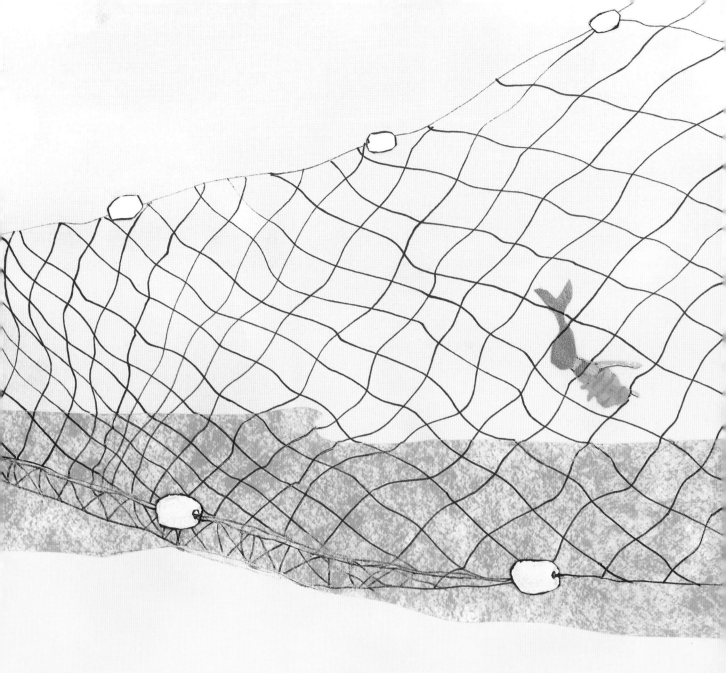

And once again Charlie is ready.

Charlie likes to be ready,

Just in case.

Charlie woke up very early today.

He's been waiting for presents and cards

And happy-birthday-to-you's since he opened his eyes.

But nobody's given him one little thing,
Not even a birthday hug,

Not even a dumb dress-up shirt or some ugly ties.

While he's feeling so sad that the whole wide world
Forgot about his birthday,

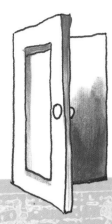

The doorbell rings,

and the house fills with girls and with guys,

Bringing birthday presents for Charlie.

Singing, "Happy birthday, dear Charlie.

We are here for your birthday party. Surprise! Surprise!"

And Charlie **isn't ready,**

He isn't the slightest bit ready,

But maybe not being ready is sometimes okay,

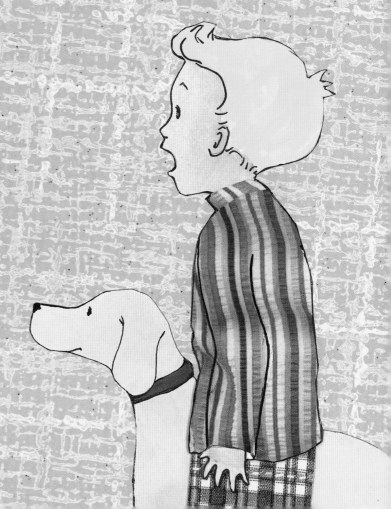

Though Charlie knows how to be ready.

And Charlie tries to be ready.

And Charlie likes to be ready,

Just in case.